COSMIC
COUNTDOWN

PUFFIN BOOKS

Published by the Penguin Group
Penguin Books Ltd, 80 Strand, London WC2R 0RL, England
Penguin Group (USA) Inc., 375 Hudson Street, New York, New York 10014,
USA Penguin Group (Canada), 90 Eglinton Avenue East, Suite 700,
Toronto, Ontario, Canada M4P 2Y3
Penguin Ireland, 25 St Stephen's Green, Dublin 2, Ireland
(a division of Penguin Books Ltd)
Penguin Group (Australia), 707 Collins Street, Melbourne, Victoria 3008, Australia
Penguin Books India Pvt Ltd, 11 Community Centre, Panchsheel Park,
New Delhi – 110 017, India
Penguin Group (NZ), 67 Apollo Drive, Rosedale, Auckland 0632, New Zealand
Penguin Books (South Africa) (Pty) Ltd, Block D, Rosebank Office Park,
181 Jan Smuts Avenue, Parktown North, Gauteng 2193, South Africa

Penguin Books Ltd, Registered Offices: 80 Strand, London WC2R 0RL, England

puffinbooks.com

First published 2014
001

Written by Sue Behrent
Illustrations by Abigail Ryder

Text and illustrations copyright © Mind Candy Ltd, 2014
Moshi Monsters is a trademark of Mind Candy Ltd. All rights reserved

The moral right of the author and illustrator has been asserted

Set in Adobe Garamond Pro
Printed in Great Britain by Clays Ltd, St Ives plc

British Library Cataloguing in Publication Data
A CIP catalogue record for this book is available from the British Library

ISBN: 978–0–141–35187–2

MIX
Paper from
responsible sources
FSC
www.fsc.org   FSC® C018179

COSMIC COUNTDOWN

T. SHREWMAN

PUFFIN

CONTENTS

Chapter 1

CRASH LANDING

As the *Rhapsody 2* disappeared completely from view, the Super Moshis and fluffy Moshling Scarlet O'Haira sighed helplessly and slumped to the floor of the escape pod.

'Now that Dr. Strangeglove has gained control of the Zoshlings' ship, who's going to investigate the mysterious star that's threatening our world?' Luvli asked anxiously. 'We're running out of time! Remember what Captain Squirk said? If the ice on Mount Sillimanjaro carries on melting so quickly, it'll only be a matter of days before Monstro City is underwater!'

Katsuma and Poppet frowned. There was nothing they could do to help either the Zoshlings or the Moshi world in their current predicament.

'This escape pod has no steering controls!' Katsuma growled in frustration.

'Er, what do you mean?' asked Poppet nervously, but Katsuma had no time to answer.

'Yeah, and if that wasn't bad enough, we're gonna smash into this huge asteroid,' moaned Furi, pointing at a huge rock ahead of them. 'Talk about having a bad day!'

'*W-w-what?*' Poppet raced over to him and gasped as the cratered surface of the asteroid approached at

top speed. 'Perplexing planetoids, Furi's right! Guys, things are about to get bumpy! We've got five seconds to execute a team huddle position.'

FIVE!

The Super Moshis and Scarlet flattened themselves to the floor.

FOUR!

They grabbed each others' hands.

THREE!

They closed their eyes tight.

TWO!

They held their breath.

BOOOOOOOM!

Diavlo opened his eyes and looked around at the tangle of wires and bits of broken metal strewn all over the escape pod.

'Is everyone OK?' he asked, dragging himself to his feet and dusting himself down. He could hear spluttery coughs and moans around the escape pod.

'All good here!' Furi groaned.

'Luvli and I are OK too,' Poppet said, wincing.

Suddenly a horrified cry filled the pod.

'Oh, duuuuude! I've lost an eye!' shrieked Zommer,

dropping to his knees to scrabble through the wreckage.

'But you've only ever had one eye, Zom,' Katsuma said, patting him on the shoulder.

'Oh yeah . . .' Zommer said, standing up slowly and looking at his feet.

'Where's Scarlet O'Haira?' Luvli asked worriedly.

Out of the corner of her eye Poppet saw bit of plastic from the escape pod's console shuffling across the floor. She lifted it up and smiled. Scarlet was underneath it.

'Yeah, Scarlet is safe too,' Poppet said.

'Great! Well . . . that could've been a lot worse!' Katsuma said, grinning. 'The only problem appears to be the sound on the communication screen.'

The Supers looked up at it. There was Captain Squirk, looking concerned and mouthing words they couldn't hear.

'We! Can't! Hear! You! Dude!' Furi yelled at the top of his lungs.

Poppet sighed loudly.

'Let's just fix the volume button, shall we?' said Luvli.

'Are you receiving me, Super Moshis?'

Captain Squirk's melodic voice filled the escape pod as Katsuma slotted the final TV fuse back into place. 'Is anybody hurt?'

'We're receiving you, Captain,' Diavlo reassured him.

'Everyone here is OK and the escape pod has only minor damage,' Poppet added. 'So if you could just tell us how to get off this rock . . . ?'

'The *Rhapsody 2*'s computer scans show you've crashed on an asteroid with a highly explosive core,' Captain Squirk began.

The Super Moshis and Scarlet all gasped, before Squirk hurriedly added, 'But don't panic, the surface is quite safe!'

8

Everyone breathed out loudly.

'What I'm trying to say, badly, is that if you can figure out a way to use this core material to create an explosion beneath the escape pod, you might be able to launch it back into space,' Captain Squirk explained.

'Thanks, Captain. We'll take a look around and see what we can come up with,' Katsuma said. 'In the meantime, are you and the crew of the *Rhapsody 2* all right? What's Strangeglove up to?'

Squirk frowned.

'We're all OK. Strangeglove has locked us in my quarters,' he replied. 'The weird thing is that he hasn't altered the course I originally set for the ship – we're still heading straight for the mystery star!'

'How odd . . .' mused Poppet.

'Well, we'd better hurry up and get back to you,' said Katsuma. 'Don't worry – the Super Moshis are on the case.'

'Good luck!' said Squirk, and the screen fizzled to black.

The door to the escape pod swooshed open and the Super Moshis found themselves on the cold, dusty surface of the asteroid.

'If only we'd crash-landed on the moon,' Furi sighed, rubbing his grumbling tummy as he looked about. 'I hear that's made of cheese. The only thing here is a bunch of stupid rocks!'

'Get your facts right! They're Cosmic Rox!' someone shouted angrily behind him.

The Super Moshis jumped in alarm and spun round to find an elderly green-bearded creature frowning at them.

'What are you doing barging your way onto my asteroid?' the figure continued, furiously wagging his

finger. 'Insulting my Rox? I'm Wally Warpspeed, the world-famous Cosmic Rox miner, and these rocks aren't stupid, they are highly explosive and so rare they're worth millions of . . . well . . . Rox, so there!'

'Sorry, Mr. Warpspeed, we crash-landed,' Luvli said, fluttering her eyelashes apologetically. 'And your Cosmic Rox really are wonderful. You must have made a fortune from selling them!'

Wally Warpspeed frowned some more.

'Well, as it happens, no,' he snapped. 'I was all ready to leave with my valuable cargo when I went to take a sip of Fizzy soda and accidentally spilt some. Then, all of a sudden . . . BOOM! The Cosmic Rox exploded and blew my spaceship apart!'

He gestured over his shoulder at the wreckage of his spaceship, drifting slowly away in the distance.

'The only thing it's good for now is keeping Fizzy locked up and out of trouble!' Wally winked cheekily.

'Er . . . riiiight,' Katsuma said doubtfully. 'Well, if you wouldn't mind, we'd like to speak to Fizzy. You see, we need to create an explosion to blast our escape pod back into the Way-Outta-Sphere and Fizzy sounds like just the guy to help us.'

'Well, that would be OK, only I lost the front door handle to my ship ages ago. But if you can find it you can speak to Fizzy.' Wally shrugged. 'It should be around here somewhere.'

It was clear to the Super Moshis that all those years of mining Cosmic Rox had sent Wally Warpspeed a little nuts.

'He's got Rox up here!' Zommer whispered to Furi, tapping his forehead meaningfully.

'And his ship's in a terrible state!' cried Poppet.

The Moshis gaped at the wreckage. The explosion had sent pieces of metal flying in all directions. Happily, though, it didn't take the Supers long to find the door handle amongst the debris. They fixed it back on to the hatch, turned it and Fizzy burst out with a squeal.

'Phew, thanks!' he cried gratefully. 'I've been stuck in there forever! Wally wants to keep me locked up because I blew up his ship – which I only did once. By accident. It wasn't my fault! It's just when I mix with Cosmic Rox everything goes BOOM!'

Fizzy stopped to draw a breath and Katsuma immediately tried to get a word in before he could start talking again!

'So you're Fizzy?' he asked.

Fizzy looked round at the Super Moshis in surprise, as if he hadn't really noticed them before.

'Haha! Sorry. I've been locked in there so long I've lost my manners,' the little drink giggled. 'I'm Fizzy, the Lipsmacking Bubbly. Who are you guys?'

Log in to **MOSHIMONSTERS.COM**, click the **GOT A SECRET CODE?** button and type the **sixth word** on the **second line** on **page 126**. Your surprise free gift will appear in your treasure chest!

Chapter 2

ASTRO GREMLIN KIDNAP

'We're the Super Moshis and we've crash-landed on this asteroid,' Poppet explained. 'We need to use your fizzy talents to launch our pod back into the Way-Outta-Sphere!'

'The only problem is we'll need to gather a lot of Cosmic Rox to make an explosion powerful enough,' Katsuma added. 'Which means digging them out of the asteroid – and we just don't have that kind of time. We have to rescue our friends, the Zoshlings, from Dr. Strangeglove and C.L.O.N.C. before – '

'Whoa! Whoa!' Fizzy held up his hands. 'One thing

at a time! You can get all the Cosmic Rox you need in the mine, over there. But first we need to blast away the meteor blocking the entrance. It got lodged in there during the last meteor shower,' explained the little Moshling. 'To do that, we only need a few Cosmic Rox, and Wally definitely has some he can give you!'

'Hey!' shouted Wally, overhearing and storming over. 'You can't go around offering these strangers my Cosmic Rox, you fizzy fiend!' he snapped. 'I told you how dangerous they are! Besides, those crazy Astro Gremlins live inside and you don't want to mess with them. They stole my poor Rover and who knows what they've done to him!'

Furi swallowed loudly.

'Uh . . . what do you think they've done with him?' he asked hesitantly.

'I wouldn't be surprised if they've taken him apart piece by piece!' Wally huffed angrily.

'T-t-t-taken him apart?' Furi's fur bristled.

'Yes, of course!' Wally continued. 'Snapped his aerial! Let his tyres down! They're evil, those Astro Gremlins, EVIL!'

'Huh? Aerial? Tyres?' Diavlo asked in confusion. 'Rover isn't, like, a living breathing pet?'

Wally frowned.

'What? Oh, no!' He chuckled to himself. 'Well yes,

he is my pet, but Rover is also my transportation device. "Rover" is short for Rox-On-Vehicle-Extraterrestrial-Runabout!'

Wally suddenly looked very sad and hurriedly wiped away the tears that welled in his eyes.

'He was my only friend.'

The Super Moshis looked at each other.

'Well, if you let us into your mine, Wally, we'll bring back Rover safe and sound,' Luvli said, patting him on the back.

The lonely old creature looked at her hopefully.

'Do you really think you can?' he asked.

'Yeah, dude!' Zommer said, slapping him harder on the back. 'Unless they've totally stripped his inner wiring and used it to weave Astro Gremlin hammocks!'

'Ooooh, now that sounds comfortable!' Furi said happily. 'I do like a nice relaxing lie down in a hammo –'

'Right! So let's clear those meteorites, eh?' Katsuma said, steering Wally out of earshot and glaring at Furi and Zommer.

The Super Moshis trudged over to the entrance of the mine and looked at the giant meteorite wedged there.

'That's a lot bigger than I thought it'd be, blast it!' Katsuma said.

'Hee hee! No problem!' Fizzy gurgled happily.

Everyone set about collecting as many Cosmic Rox as they could find littered across the surface of the asteroid, then packed them into the holes of the meteorite. Fizzy, meanwhile, got into what he called 'the fizz zone' by jumping up and down on the spot.

'I'm ready, Zzzuper Moshizzzz!' he called, his bubbly tummy fizzing and spitting. 'Zzzzztand back!'

Aiming his straw at the meteorite, Fizzy let loose a jet of wizzy-fizz pink pop at the Cosmic Rox and . . .

KAAAAAAA-BOOOOOOOOOOOOOOM!

'Wow, dude, that was INSANE!' Zommer cried admiringly as the smoke and dust cleared to reveal a big hole where the meteorite had been. 'Do it again!'

'No, Zom!' said Poppet. 'We can't waste time – we'd better get into that mine. Not that I particularly want to meet those Astro Gremlins . . .'

The Moshis peered into the murky tunnel that led into the depths of the mine and shivered.

'Good luck, Super Moshis,' said Wally. 'Don't forget to rescue Rover.'

Inside, the mine was exactly as they'd imagined it to be – dark, damp and dangerous. The narrow tunnel wound down towards the asteroid's core and the Super Moshis crept along it, holding up torches Wally had given them to light their path.

'So let's play a game,' Zommer whispered in the gloom. 'I call it "Nut or Not".'

'I don't really think this is the time, Zom,' Luvli murmured quietly in reply.

'It's a gnarly game, trust me. And it'll take our minds off the Astro Gremlins,' Zommer assured her. 'I'll go first. Wally Warpspeed – nut or not?'

'Definitely nut,' Diavlo muttered.

'Mmmm, nuts,' Furi said dreamily.

'Shush!' cried Poppet. 'Did you guys hear that?'

The sound of distant barking echoed through the tunnel.

'I hope that's Rover!' Diavlo said. 'And not some kind of sick Astro Gremlin trick . . .'

'We'll soon see,' said Katsuma grimly. 'Be on your guard, everyone!'

Slowly the tunnel widened and the Supers found themselves in a large, dark cavern studded with pink glowing Cosmic Rox. And there in the middle of the rocky floor sat a very sad-looking vehicle. Its headlights were crooked, its aerial had been snapped off and it was missing its wheels, but other than that it looked unharmed.

'What is that?' said Furi, cocking his head to the side.

Bark! Bark! Bark!

They'd found Rover!

'Hello, boy!' Luvli said, floating over to the robot. 'We're the Super Moshis and we've come to rescue you.'

Rover wagged what was left of his aerial-tail and

panted happily as she patted him. Meanwhile the other Supers spread out around the cavern to examine the walls, which were pitted with holes.

Bark! Bark! Bark!

'The Astro Gremlins stole your parts, eh?' Luvli said. 'And they live in those holes in the wall!'

Furi and Zommer quickly stepped back from the

hole they'd been investigating. Suddenly a little creature with a blue face and huge, bulbous purple eyes poked its head out, chuckling cruelly.

'Yeah they do!' Zommer said, jumping with fright. They all watched as the Astro Gremlin, burbling to itself, dropped out of the hole and bustled towards Rover.

'BARK! BARK!' Rover said, flashing his wonky headlights at the Astro Gremlin. 'BARK! BARK! BARK! GRRRR-BARK!'

'Argh!' Gnashing its horrible yellow fangs, the Astro Gremlin quickly covered its eyes with its hands and raced back to the wall, disappearing into its hole.

'What did Rover say, Luvli?' Katsuma asked excitedly.

'He said that the Astro Gremlins are scared of bright

lights,' she replied. 'Unfortunately, they usually launch their attack from all sides and Rover can't flash his lights everywhere at once. That's why they've managed to run off with his parts.'

'Bright lights, eh?' Katsuma muttered thoughtfully as he looked at his fire-torch. 'I believe that's given me an idea . . .'

A few minutes later, the Super Moshis had spread out around the walls of the cavern, their fire-torches held high above their heads.

'Here's the plan,' Katsuma said. 'When an Astro Gremlin pokes its head out of a hole, shine your torch towards it! I'm hoping they'll be so startled they'll accidentally drop the missing parts they've got stashed in their hiding places.'

'Bark! Bark?' Rover asked.

'Yes, you can help too, Rover,' Luvli replied.

Sure enough, being extremely curious creatures, the

Astro Gremlins were soon sticking their heads out of their holes to see what the Super Moshis were up to. And when they saw the torch flames, they scrambled back, shrieking loudly!

Soon random things began to drop from the holes: bits of metal and wire, Cosmic Rox pebbles and more. Amongst the debris, the Supers spotted Rover's missing parts. They started putting the mechanical pet back together again.

'We still need more Cosmic Rox,' said Poppet, gathering the little pile she'd collected and putting them in her backpack. 'We'll need to get more from those pesky gremlins.'

'Stop! Please don't hurt us!' a voice cried behind her.

The Super Moshis turned to see an Astro Gremlin cowering nearby.

'We're sorry! We'll do anything you want if you'll only stop waving those torches!' it pleaded as it squinted at them.

'We need heaps of Cosmic Rox,' Poppet said. 'Do you have any stashed around here?'

'Yes, plenty!' the Astro Gremlin replied. 'Take as many as you like – just go back to the surface where you belong!'

'And we're taking Rover with us,' Diavlo said, waving his torch menacingly.

'Yes! YES! Whatever you like!' said the Astro Gremlin, hastily shielding his eyes.

'Well, that's settled then!' Luvli smiled as she extinguished her torch.

Chapter 3

COSMIC ROX LIFT-OFF

The Astro Gremlins cooperated, much to the Super Moshis' surprise. Not only did they give the Supers their secret stash of Cosmic Rox, but they used their own makeshift mine carts to transport the Rox back through the tunnel!

'We can go no further,' the Astro Gremlin said, pointing to the bright light at the end of the tunnel. 'We cannot go to the surface.'

'There's no need. You've done your part and we appreciate your help,' Poppet said. 'Thank you.'

'Bark! Bark!' Rover added.

'He's saying goodbye,' Luvli said, smiling.

The Astro Gremlin looked at Rover and then reached out cautiously to pat him.

'Aw, look at that,' Furi cooed as the Astro Gremlin carefully stroked Rover's back. 'They're friends now.'

But the naughty creature suddenly reached for Rover's aerial-tail and gave it a sharp tug.

'Stop it, dude! That's way uncool. We've only just put Rover back together again!' Zommer said, flapping his arms to shoo away the Astro Gremlin.

With a high-pitched screech all the Astro Gremlins scattered, disappearing back down into the depths of the mine.

The Super Moshis emerged to find Wally waiting expectantly at the mine entrance, wringing his hands.

'I thought I heard barking!' he exclaimed, jumping high in the air as he spotted his pet. 'ROVER!' He raced over to hug his best friend. 'I didn't think I'd ever see you again!'

As the two old friends exchanged barks and more hugs, Fizzy happily jumped up and down on top of the pile of Cosmic Rox they'd gathered.

'Wowzers! You guys should go into the mining business!' he cried, scampering up to the top of the heap. 'It looks like you've got a talent for sniffing out Cosmic Rox!'

Katsuma grimaced. 'Er . . . Fizzy? Would you mind getting down off there?' he said. 'We don't want another accident.'

Fizzy giggled nervously and carefully climbed down. 'Oh! Yeah, yeah, of course.'

It was dusty and difficult work, but with the help of Rover and Wally (who, now that the Supers had rescued his friend, appeared to have completely forgotten he didn't trust them!) the adventurers managed to pile the huge heap of Cosmic Rox under their escape pod.

'Phew! That was exhausting!' Furi moaned as he collapsed on the ground, panting. 'I'd never have believed carrying Rox back and forth could be so tiring!'

'Yeah, totally!' Zommer agreed, shaking Rox dust out of his spiky hair. 'Radical respect, Wally – you've got a killer job, dude!'

Wally blushed shyly.

'Thank you,' he said, grinning. 'And I didn't believe you'd be able to defeat those mischievous Astro Gremlins and get my Rover back.'

'Y'know, Wally, they're not so bad,' Diavlo said. 'The Astro Gremlins did give us their Cosmic Rox and help us transport them to the surface.'

'Just don't ever let them dog-sit Rover!' Luvli laughed. 'They'll strip him of metal quicker than you can say "demolish and polish".'

'BARK! BARK!' Rover nodded in agreement.

'Well, I guess we'd better climb aboard the escape pod and get going,' Poppet said. 'We still have to rescue our Zoshling friends. And there's that little matter of the ever-expanding star that needs investigating!'

Everyone looked up at the huge star that now outshone all the others in the Swooniverse.

'Ahem!' Fizzy coughed meaningfully. 'Perhaps I could tag along? Who knows, you might need my wizzy-fizz pop again . . .'

Katsuma smiled. 'Absolutely! We've had a lot of

help from Moshlings on our adventures!' he said.

'Exzzzzellent!' Fizzy frothed gleefully.

The Supers and Fizzy said farewell to Wally and Rover and climbed through the hatch of the escape pod, where Scarlett O'Haira was waiting with fluffy hugs for everyone.

Even though Wally was kind of a grouch, the Supers were sad to leave their new friends behind. But the old Cosmic Rox miner wanted to follow his dreams of striking it rich . . . and, who knows, with Rover to help him maybe he'd do it!

Poppet set about figuring out the best course to reach the *Rhapsody 2*. The ship had been heading for the giant star, so she decided that's where the Super Moshis should head too! The rest of the Supers were watching expectantly as Fizzy got into the 'fizz zone'.

'Trajectory set!' Poppet hollered.

'I'm zzzzzzzuper ready!' Fizzy buzzed, and with a

squirt of his wizzy-fizz pop the Cosmic Rox exploded, launching the escape pod off the asteroid and into the Way-Outta-Sphere!

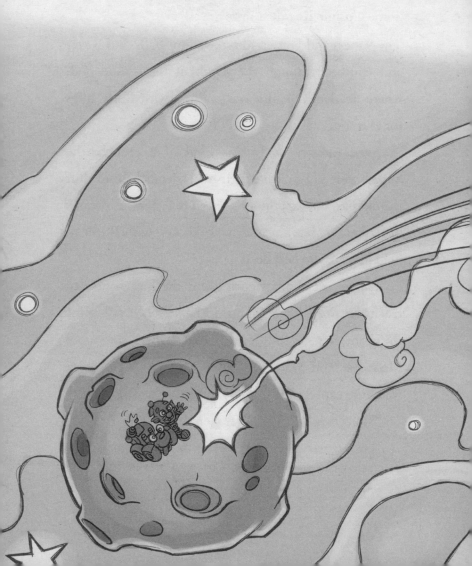

Down below on the asteroid Wally rubbed his eyes.

'Bark! Bark?' Rover asked in disbelief.

'No, I'm not crying!' Wally snapped. 'I've just got some Cosmic Rox dust in my eyes!'

'We're approaching the mystery star!' Poppet called, pointing. 'Come and see!'

The Supers and Moshlings raced over and peered out into space.

'It's huge!' Furi yelped.

'It's enormous!' Luvli exclaimed.

'Jumping Jupiter! It's . . . it's not a star!' Katsuma shouted. 'It's C.L.O.N.C.'s space-base!'

'Epic! How do you figure that?' Zommer asked, pressing his face to the glass.

'Um . . . well . . . the sign that says "C.L.O.N.C." is kind of a giveaway,' Katsuma replied, pointing to the flickering neon in the distance.

'And look! They've sent out a welcoming party! Glumpanauts!' Poppet cried.

'I've got this one, Poppet!' Zommer yelled as he raced to the weapon control panel and fired up the escape pod's blaster. 'I nailed Hoodoo Pong in the Unknown Zone and the Arcade Machine on the *Rhapsody 2*. I don't think a few spaced-out Glumps will be a problem.'

Everyone watched anxiously as the Glumpanauts approached.

'Go, Gamesmeister!' Furi cheered as the others held their breath.

Zommer let loose with a blast of goo-brew that splattered the helmets of the Glumpanauts with pink gloop, which

left them totally unable to see where they were flying.

'Look! They're out of control and crashing into each other!' Fizzy shrieked as a Glumpanaut narrowly missed the escape pod. 'I hope they don't hit us!'

'Don't worry, Fizzy, we're floating out of range,' Katsuma said as they ran to the opposite side of the capsule to watch the blundering Glumps flying round in circles.

'Out of range of the Glumpanauts, yes,' Luvli said, swallowing nervously. 'But we're heading right for the hangar bay of C.L.O.N.C.'s space base . . . '

With no way to steer the escape pod, the Supers could only watch helplessly as it drifted into C.L.O.N.C.'s lair.

'We're done for this time,' Furi growled. 'But Strangeglove and his C.L.O.N.C. cronies won't take us without a fight! Oh no, we'll be ready and waiting!'

But as the escape pod bounced to a halt on the floor of the hangar, they could only see Sprockett and Hubbs waiting for them. The *Rhapsody 2* was parked behind them, deserted.

The Supers raced out of the capsule.

'What are you two doing here?' asked Diavlo suspiciously. 'And where are the Zoshlings?'

'Super Moshis! The Zoshlings have been captured and imprisoned by C.L.O.N.C.!' Hubbs blurted out.

'Our scanners indicate they're being held in Cell Block F,' Sprockett added. 'You have to save them!'

Chapter 4

THE C.L.O.N.C. SPACE BASE

Now Katsuma's eyes narrowed suspiciously. 'Why didn't you guys get captured?' he asked.

'We hid with the tin cans in the trash pile,' Hubbs explained. 'Why don't you trust us?'

'Well . . .' Luvli began hesitantly.

'Look, we don't have time for this!' Sprockett said hurriedly. 'You have to get out of here before any Glump guards show up. C.L.O.N.C. will have spotted your ship on the space-base scanners and you can bet they'll try anything to stop you from rescuing Captain Squirk and his crew.'

'Sprockett is right, guys,' Zommer said.

Luvli, Furi and Diavlo nodded in agreement.

'OK, OK,' Luvli huffed, turning to Sprockett and Hubbs. 'Show us how to get into Cell Block F. But if you try any tricks, the pair of you will end up on the pointy end of an Up and Away Whirl!'

'Fine!' Hubbs said, rolling his robot eyes. 'But from now on no talking. There's a Glump sentry stationed

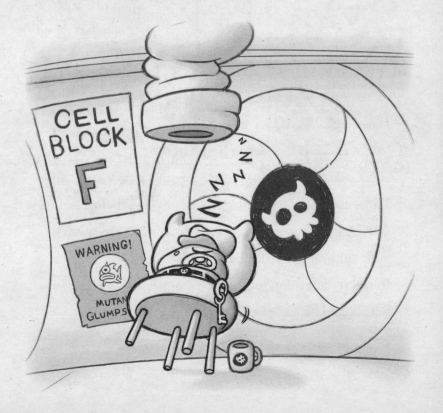

at the door to Cell Block F and we don't want any trouble if we can avoid it.'

'Speak for yourself,' Furi grinned, cracking his knuckles menacingly. 'I'd quite like some trouble.'

'Yeah! I'd like a gnarly helping of trouble with a side order of punch-in-the-face,' Zommer giggled.

'Punch-in-the-face? Is that like Toad in the Hole?' Hubbs smirked.

'Dunno! Wanna try some and find out?' Zommer said, balling his fists.

'Hey, guuuys! No fighting amongst ourselves, OK?' Poppet cried. 'The evil atmosphere on C.L.O.N.C.'s space base is making us all a little crazy. So relax.'

Hubbs and Zommer hung their heads.

'Sorry, Hubbs,' Zommer mumbled, holding out his gloved hand.

'Yeah, I'm sorry too, Zommer,' Hubbs replied, shaking it.

'Cosmic crumbs! Now can we go and rescue some Zoshlings?' Katsuma sighed.

The Supers and the robots crept silently across the hangar and hid behind a pile of drums stacked in a far corner. From there they had a perfect view of the doors to Cell Block F . . . and the Glump guard snoozing on the job.

'Typical Glump,' Diavlo muttered.

The Glump guard wriggled uncomfortably in his seat.

Sprockett turned to Diavlo and put his finger over his electronic mouth. 'Shhhh,' he whispered.

Meanwhile, Hubbs had spotted something clipped to the Glump's belt – a key! But how could he tell the Supers without making a noise? Why, CHARADES of course!

For the next few minutes Hubbs tried his hardest to mime turning a key in a lock, but the Supers didn't get it. Furi thought he was signalling making a hole in a doughnut.

Next he tried to mime 'sounds like key', but Luvli thought he was being a bee, Poppet thought he was having a cup of tea and Zommer thought he was trying to ski!

Hubbs threw his arms up in the air in frustration.
'A key,' he hissed.

'Dude, I was just going to say that!' Zommer said, slapping his forehead.

'Shhhhh!' Sprockett hushed loudly.

'Everyone. Shut. Up!' Katsuma snapped.

Poppet peeked out from behind the pile of drums and saw that the Glump was still napping. She was just wondering how they could get the key from him when she noticed a large tube right above where the Glump was slumped in his chair. It said 'SUCK' next to the tube and leading out of it were two pipes with buttons set rather far apart.

Poppet grinned – she'd just worked out how they could get the key!

'So, we're just going to hoover him up?' Luvli whispered excitedly.

Poppet nodded.

'Can you help us with that tube?' Poppet asked Hubbs. His rollerball wheel would allow him to move silently across the floor without disturbing the guard.

'My scan shows a complex mechanism that could require a complete rework of the system!' cried the robot in reply.

'Or you can hold one button down while I press the other? That's what powers the sucking mechanism, according to my scan,' offered Sprockett.

Hubbs glared at him.

'Yeah, that'll work too . . . but are you sure you want me to do it? My wheel sometimes squeaks a bit and it might wake up the guard . . .'

'Don't worry. There's plenty of oil in these if we need it,' Katsuma replied quietly, patting the stack of drums.

'These drums don't have oil in them, Katsuma,' Furi said. 'They're full of de-glumping goo. Look, it's written on the side.'

'Doesn't matter. I'm sure you'll be fine,' Diavlo said, shoving the little robot out from behind the wall of drums.

Hubbs looked back nervously for a moment then scooted noiselessly across the floor, Sprockett hurrying behind. They stationed themselves next to the two pipes, nodded, then punched the buttons.

SWOOOOOOOOOOOOOOOOOOCH!

It sounded like someone noisily slurping Gloop Soup! The slumbering Glump never stood a chance. He was still half asleep as the tube sucked him out of his chair. The key fell away from his belt, dropping to the floor with a tinkle.

The Super Moshis
raced over to grab the
key and quickly opened
the door to Cell Block
F. And who should
be standing right
inside the entrance,
but Gabby the Mini
Moshifone!

'Gabby!' cried
Poppet, running
towards one of her favourite Moshlings.

'We're saved!' the little Moshifone cried with relief,
jumping into Poppet's arms. 'I was able to escape, but
there are hundreds of Moshlings still trapped in there,
and they're well guarded by Mutant Glump Sharks!'

'Wait! Back up a bit. What other Moshlings?'
Katsuma asked.

'C.L.O.N.C. has been kidnapping Moshlings and
turning them into Glumps,' Gabby explained tearfully.

'They plan to build a huge Glump army to destroy the Moshi World.'

'It's OK now, Gabby,' Poppet said soothingly, but her eyes flashed with fury. 'The Super Moshis are here.'

Luvli turned to Hubbs.

'What about these Mutant Glump Sharks? Can we beat them?' she asked.

'They're vicious and difficult to destroy,' Hubbs replied. 'What we need is . . .'

'De-glumping goo!' Sprockett shouted excitedly.

'Yeah, that'd be good,' Hubbs said with a long-suffering sigh. 'I'll just pop down the shop and get some, shall I? You bubble-headed bag of bolts, where do you think –'

'Great idea, Sprockett!' Diavlo said, cutting him off. 'The drums we were hiding behind – Furi said they were full of de-glumping goo!'

'Yeah, good thinking, Sprockett!' Katsuma chimed in. 'If we fill the escape pod's blaster with the goo, we'll be able to fly right into Cell Block F and take those Mutant Glump Sharks apart!'

'Radical!' Zommer cried. 'Let's lock and load, Super Moshis!'

The Supers immediately swung into action!

Poppet placed Gabby carefully in the *Rhapsody 2* with Scarlet O'Haira and told the little Moshlings to look after each other.

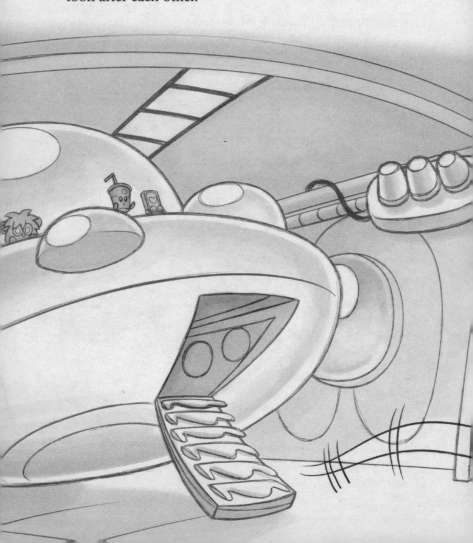

Meanwhile, the others quickly loaded up the blaster with de-glumping goo – and in no time they were ready to face the Mutant Glump Sharks.

'Come and get us, fishy fishy!' Diavlo bellowed as the door to Cell Block F whooshed open and the Super Moshis flew inside.

Chapter 5

GLOOPING MUTANT GLUMP SHARKS

'There are zillions of them!' Luvli cried as the Mutant Glump Sharks swarmed around the escape pod, pressing their googly eyes against the glass.

'Urgh! They're gross!' Poppet said, stepping back as an orange Glump Shark with a gaping dribbly mouth smeared its gunge across the window.

'Hey! Look at those armoured pods,' Katsuma said, pointing to the four large metal orbs floating around the cellblock. 'I bet that's where C.L.O.N.C. are keeping the Moshlings locked up.'

'I can't see anything but Mutant Glump Shark eyes!' Diavlo moaned.

'Well, hold on to your masks, Supers, cos it's de-glumping time!' Zommer laughed as he opened fire with the escape pod's blaster.

PYEW! PYEW! PYEW! PYEW! PYEW! PYEW!

As each Mutant Glump Shark took a faceful of de-glumping goo, it transformed back into a cute, harmless Moshling!

'Terrific transformations! Are you seeing what I'm seeing, Zom?' Furi yelled in wonder.

'I am, dude, I totally am!' Zommer whooped.

PYEW! PYEW! PYEW! PYEW! PYEW! PYEW!

Soon all the Mutant Glump Sharks had disappeared, replaced by Big Mouth Squiddly Dees, Brassy Blowy Things, Oochie Poochies and a zillion other adorable creatures!

'Now to free the Moshlings that are locked up in those orbs,' Poppet said. 'Fire when ready, Zom.'

PYEW! PYEW! PYEW! PYEW! PYEW! PYEW!

Two orbs immediately broke open like eggs, sending happy Moshlings scattering in all directions.

But the other two – one dazzlingly white, the other all wrapped up in chains – proved much more difficult to crack!

The escape pod drifted close to the white one and the Supers peered at it.

'It looks like it's . . .' Luvli's voice trailed off.

'. . . made of snow?' Furi said.

'I see a hole where the de-glumping goo has melted some ice. Diavlo, take the escape pod in there,' Poppet called before adding under her breath, 'I hope we don't find a bunch of Moshling ice lollies in there.'

It was colder than eating an Ice Scream on the Frostipop Glacier inside that icy orb. In other words, it was just the right temperature for Tomba the Wistful Snowtot!

'Oh hey, Super Moshis,' said the Moshling sadly as they piled out of the escape pod. 'Have you been locked up in here too? I don't think we're ever getting out.'

'Actually we're here to rescue you, Tomba,' Katsuma said, smiling.

'And your friend over here,' Poppet added as she peered into a square block of ice in the middle of the chamber. 'Whoever it is!'

'It's Judder, the Unhinged Jackhammer,' Tomba

replied miserably, looking at the Moshling frozen stiff.
'C.L.O.N.C. put him in ICE-olation because he kept
breaking things.'

'That's cold, man. That's real cold,' Zommer winced.

'Do you seriously think you can rescue us?' Tomba
asked, a tiny glimmer of hope in his voice.

'Yeah, of course!' Diavlo cried. 'But first things first. We need to get some heat going in here. My lava-head is frosting over!'

'The heater is up there,' said Tomba, pointing to a control panel near the ceiling. 'But it's broken, of course.'

'Let me take a look,' Luvli said brightly as she flew up to investigate the heater. 'Oh, it's missing the pointer that sets the temperature,' she called back. 'That's easily fixed.'

'Is it?' Tomba moaned. 'It doesn't look very easy to me.'

Luvli flew back down, landing beside the grumbly Moshling.

'I can do it with your help,' she smiled.

'Really?' Tomba asked.

'Really! I just need to borrow your pointy nose for a moment,' she replied.

Tomba plucked off his little carrot nose and handed it to Luvli, who immediately flew up to the

heater and
attached it to the
control panel. It
looked just like
the pointer that
was missing!

'Now I just
turn up the
heat,' she said,
grinning. She
turned the carrot tip to point at an image of a melting
Glump. 'And we wait for the ice to melt!'

'Is anyone else hungry?' Furi asked suddenly.

'I'm a bit peckish,' Katsuma admitted. 'Why?'

'It seems this orb wasn't only for keeping Moshlings
on ice.' Furi replied, his voice rising in excitement. 'It's
C.L.O.N.C.'s refrigerator!'

The Super Moshis looked around and saw that
Furi was right. The ice was beginning to melt and they
could already see a chicken defrosting, along with some

peas, a large packet of noodles and, luckily, a stove.

'Helloooooo chicken soup!' Furi said, smacking his lips.

The Supers kept a watchful eye on Judder while they set about making the food.

'Are you OK, little guy?' asked Poppet.

'N-n-n-no!' shuddered the Moshling. 'I think I've cau-cau-caught the flu! I feel terrible.'

Poppet frowned in concern.

'Oh no! Well, the chicken soup Furi is cooking will make you feel much better,' she said.

Once Furi had simmered the delicious smelling soup on the stove for a while, Luvli poured a bowl for Judder and fed him some.

'Are you feeling better now?' Katsuma asked as the icicles hanging from the Unhinged Jackhammer's handles began to evaporate.

'M-m-m-much better thanks to you g-g-g-g-guys!'

Judder grinned. 'I just need to w-w-w-warm up a bit more. Jumping on the s-s-s-s-spot should help!'

The manic Moshling suddenly began hammering all around the orb, shattering everything in its path!

'Whoa! Watch out for the hot pot, dude!' Zommer laughed as Judder bounced past it.

'So how did you get here, Tomba?' Poppet asked, putting the carrot back on the Moshling's face.

'I don't really know,' Tomba replied forlornly. 'One minute I was chilling out on Mount Sillimanjaro, then this bright light appeared. Next thing I know, I'm here.'

'If only we knew where the Zoshlings were being kept . . .' Luvli frowned.

'E-e-e-easy!' Judder replied as he zipped by. 'They're being held in the cell block next to us!'

'What? The one locked up tight with chains and keys and stuff?' Furi asked. 'I don't see how we can get past all that security.'

Judder rolled his eyes . . . or maybe they were just boinging around in his head – it was hard to tell!

'L-l-l-leave it to me, Super M-m-m-moshis!' he chuckled as he drilled his way out through the floor.

'I wish Judder had told us he was going to do that,' Katsuma sighed. 'I'm pretty sure there's gonna be more Mutant Glump Sharks circling out there and he has no way of defending himself!'

'Then we'd better go too!' Poppet said.

The Super Moshis and Tomba raced over to the escape pod and piled inside. Diavlo gunned the engine and they sped out of the orb.

Zommer and Furi looked back at the complete mess Judder had made as they zipped outside.

'Even though he's a friendly little dude, I can kinda

see why C.L.O.N.C. froze him,' Zommer whispered.

'He certainly knows how to break the ice . . .' Furi snickered.

Zommer high-fived him.

Chapter 6

THE SQUEAL OF FORTUNE

As soon as the escape pod moved out into the Cell Block a new batch of Mutant Glump Sharks launched their attack. Luckily there was plenty of de-glumping goo left in the pod's blaster!

PYEW! PYEW! PYEW! PYEW! PYEW! PYEW!

And soon all the Mutant Glump Sharks had been transformed back into loveable Moshlings.

'Look!' cried Diavlo. 'There's Judder – and he's OK!'

The Super Moshis looked to where he was pointing. Judder wasn't only OK, he was making short work of hammering through the chains locked around the orb containing the Zoshlings!

'He's through!' Luvli cried as the last of the chains
fell to the hangar floor.

'Then hold tight, everyone. We're going in!' Diavlo
cried as the escape pod moved towards the hole Judder
had made in the final orb.

'What terrible trick is C.L.O.N.C. playing now?' Diavlo exclaimed as the Super Moshis walked out of the escape pod.

The four Zoshlings were inside the orb all right, but they were trapped inside bright beams of light that spluttered and buzzed with electricity.

'Don't worry,' Furi murmured, cracking his knuckles.

'There's only one measly Glump guarding them.'

At the sound of voices the Glump turned round.

'Security alert!' it shouted. 'What are you doing here?'

'Er . . . we're not intruders . . . we've just started working for C.L.O.N.C.,' Katsuma replied quickly.

'Well, if you're new to the team, that means only one thing!' cried the Glump.

The Moshis looked at each other, confused, as the set of a glitzy TV game show rolled into a view.

'You have to play "SQUEEEEEEEEEEEEEEAL OF FORTUNE!" And I'm your handsome host, Knowledge Head Ned.'

'Jumping jellyfat! We're on telly?' Zommer exclaimed.

'That's riiiiiight!' Ned cried. 'And we have some wonderful prizes. There's four – count em, FOUR – Zoshliiiiiiiiiiiiiiiiings up for grabs!'

'Wow, this is revolting even by C.L.O.N.C. standards,' Poppet grumbled.

'OK, let's get this over and done with,' Katsuma

said gruffly. 'I nominate me. I'll play this "Squeal of Fortune."' He narrowed his eyes and stepped forward.

Like every game show in the Swooniverse and beyond, the aim of the game was to answer questions and win prizes. But in this case the 'prizes' were the Zoshlings!

'Welcome, my furry friend,' said Ned, adjusting his square glasses and grinning with a gap-toothed smile. 'And what is your name?'

'Um . . . Super Woshi?' said Katsuma, looking back at the Moshis with an awkward shrug.

'Hello, Super Woshi!' said Ned, unbothered by the suspicious name. 'Great to have you with us! Now, to win these special prizes – he indicated the poor trapped Zoshlings – 'simply answer four simple questions, all about C.L.O.N.C., and unscramble the secret password!'

Now, luckily for the galactic globetrotting Zoshlings, the Super Moshis knew a lot about C.L.O.N.C., especially from all their missions on Music Island. Katsuma smiled craftily as Ned began.

'First question. What was the name of the hotel that Frau Now BraunKau was stationed at?'

Katsuma crossed his arms. 'Easy – The Sandy Drain Hotel,' he said. None of the Supers would easily forget rescuing Zack Binspin and Rofl from that crazy cow at the gooperstar hotel.

'Corrrrrrect!' said Ned, winking at the non-existent camera. The Super Moshis screamed with delight. 'And you have also revealed four letters from the password.' He pointed to a board containing nine blank squares. Suddenly, four of them turned to show the letter 'S'.

'Four Ss?' said Luvli, scratching her head.

'Next question!' cried Ned, straightening his tie and winking again. 'You find Mr. Snoodle onboard the C.L.O.N.C. star. What do you do?'

Katsuma knew the answer to this one too. They all did. It wasn't what the Moshis would do to Moshlings, but unfortunately it's what evil C.L.O.N.C. would do.

'Put that Moshling in the Glumpatron 3000!' he said, faking an evil laugh.

Poppet grimaced. It wasn't nice pretending to be cruel to Moshlings.

'That's right! And you have another letter – an R!' yelled Ned excitedly. 'Now, third question! Which C.L.O.N.C. operative went undercover at the Cirque du Bonbon?'

Katsuma smiled. That was easy. Who could forget the silly squeaky villain they'd unmasked at the circus?

'Sweet Tooth,' said Katsuma, rubbing his paws.

'My favourite agent!' shouted Ned.

'Er, yeah, mine too,' said Katsuma.

'You just got an "F". And that brings us to our fourth and final question!' said Ned, waggling his hideous eyebrows at the Moshi audience. 'You want to buy something at Yukea, but you don't have enough Rox. What do you do?'

Now, Katsuma was a good, upstanding Moshi. He had never committed a crime in his life. But he knew what C.L.O.N.C. would do – and what he had to say to win the game. He clenched his teeth.

'I would steal it,' he said.

Ned leapt down from his stage. 'That's right! An amazing display of C.L.O.N.C. knowledge! Here are those final letters – two As! Can you unscramble the secret password and release those Zoshling prizes?' teased Ned.

Katsuma looked at the letters for a few moments, trying out different combinations in his head. Only one word sounded right, although it also sounded kind of silly.

'Sassafras?' he said, unsure.

Ned jumped in the air with a yelp. 'You got it, buddy!' he cried. 'The most fearsome and cruel naval master onboard. Commander Sassafras!'

The beams of light holding the Zoshlings disappeared and they floated softly to the floor. Poppet and Luvli raced over to fetch them.

'Stupid name, Sassafras,' whispered Zommer to Furi, who nodded in agreement.

But Ned wasn't finished. 'And, boy, do we have a treat for you tonight! 'Here he is! Joining us liiiiiiiiiive onstage – Commander Sassafras himself!'

Suddenly the hatch to the orb whooshed open and a floating ship with a terrifying-looking captain at the helm started moving at speed towards them. His hat

was trimmed with feathers and his jacket was heavy
with gold braid and medals he'd won for his dastardly
deeds. On the front of his ship was a huge cannon and
it was pointed straight at the Supers!

'Not so stupid now!' yelled Diavlo. 'Let's get to the
escape pod before Sassafras gets to us!'

The Super Moshis raced towards their capsule with the Zoshlings, slamming the door shut just as Commander Sassafras's ship opened fire.

BOOM! BOOM! BOOM!

'I got this!' cried Zommer. 'Starting engines! Hold tight, everyone, things are gonna get a little crazy!'

The escape pod rose into the air and flew straight at Sassafras, its blaster spewing forth de-glumping goo.

PYEW! PYEW! PYEW! PYEW! PYEW! PYEW! BOOM! BOOM!

Every cannonball that hit the escape pod sent shudders through its passengers.

'C'mon, Zom!' Furi yelled over the noise. 'You've got to take down Commander Cuckoo before the pod blows apart!'

PYEW! PYEW! PYEW! PYEW! PYEW! PYEW! BOOM! BOOM!

Through the porthole the Supers and the Zoshlings watched as de-glumping goo coated Sassafras's ship in pink gunge.

'Epic! Sassy-pants is flying off course!' Zommer whooped gleefully. 'He can't see a thing through that thick layer of de-glumping goo!'

'And he can't see to fire his cannons either!' Poppet shouted happily.

'ABANDON SHIP!' Commander Sassafras

shrieked as his craft spiralled out of control, crashing into the wall of the orb.

'We're saved!' Luvli cheered.

'MWAHAHAHAHA! Not so fast, icky sticky glooper Moshis!' Without warning, the moustachioed face of Dr. Strangeglove filled the escape pod's communication screen. Behind him the Supers glimpsed Sweet Tooth, Big Chief Tiny Head, Frau Now BrownKau and other C.L.O.N.C. agents smirking triumphantly. 'Saving Zoshlings is one thing, but defeating C.L.O.N.C.? I don't think so!'

'SILENCE STRANGEGLOVE!' an angry voice suddenly boomed out. The Moshis looked at each other in astonishment. It couldn't be . . . it had to be . . . the Boss of C.L.O.N.C.? So this evil plan went higher than Strangeglove – all the way to the top?

The monsters watched with bated breath as the C.L.O.N.C. agents hurriedly stepped aside to reveal the Boss . . . hidden behind an enormous armchair. All they could see was an angry fist shaking at Strangeglove.

'You're lucky to even be here, you fool! Step aside. It's time to witness my greatest triumph – the destruction of the entire Moshi World!' he roared.

The screen switched to a view of the Swooniverse outside the space base. Everything looked normal at first. There was the sun, smiling happily. But suddenly a giant magnifying glass strapped to a satellite moved into view.

'No!' cried Katsuma. 'When the sun's rays hit that

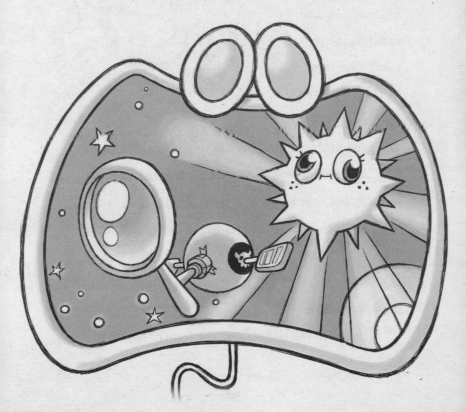

magnifying glass, they'll be converted into a beam of light equivalent to a trillion suns. And that beam is headed straight for the Moshi World!

'Hahaha, that's right, you overgrown furball!' said the Boss. 'The Trubble Satellite's Deluxe Doom Ray 5000 will melt Sillimanjaro and flood Monstro City! Your kind will be DESTROYED!' He chortled evilly

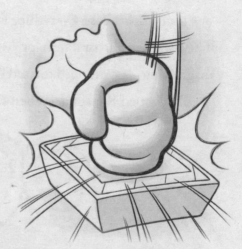

and pressed the big red button to activate the Doom Ray. 'Any second, my C.L.O.N.C. companions, any second, and that beam of – wait. What's this?'

The Boss scowled and slammed his fist on his chair. The word 'LOADING' was blinking on the screen.

'Doom Ray at 5%?' he roared furiously. 'Blast this slow connection!

The screen clicked off and the Super Moshis looked

at each other, determination in their eyes.

'Right! This buys us a bit of time,' said Poppet. First thing to do is switch off that Doom Ray! Ideas, anyone?'

First Officer Ooze cleared his throat meaningfully and elbowed Splutnik in the ribs.

'Oh! Yes,' said Splutnik. 'When C.L.O.N.C. captured our ship, we ran a scan of the entire base on our equipment – just before those villains grabbed us and threw us in this prison. If we can get back to the *Rhapsody 2*, we can look at the scan and find out where the weapon's control centre is.'

'Well, what are we waiting for? A written invitation from C.L.O.N.C.?' Diavlo said, leading the way.

On the bridge of the space base, the Boss glared silently at his C.L.O.N.C. underlings. The painfully slow computer connection had made him even angrier than usual. And that was very angry indeed!

'If I know those Super Snoopers, they won't give up

without a fight!' the Boss snarled.

'Let me go after them, Boss,' Strangeglove volunteered eagerly. 'I'll crush them –'

'Shut up!' the Boss thundered. 'You've disappointed me too many times, Strangeglove! Sweet Tooth, Big

Chief Tiny Head? You must stop them . . . once and for all!'

'No worry. You count on us,' Big Chief replied, his voice tinged with fear.

It was never a good idea to disappoint the Boss . . .

Meanwhile the Super Moshis and the Zoshlings had returned to the *Rhapsody 2*, where Sprockett and Hubbs were waiting eagerly.

'The Moshlings you rescued are all safely aboard the ship, Captain Squirk,' Hubbs said. 'Including Tomba, Judder, Fizzy and Scarlet O'Haira.'

'We're ready to return to Moshi World just as soon as you are,' Sprockett added.

'You're imposters!' Zommer cried accusingly, pointing at the robots. 'What have you done with the real Sprockett and Hubbs?'

'Huh? What do you mean, Zom?' Katsuma asked, confused.

'These ex-C.L.O.N.C. agents that we know and, well, quite like I guess, would never care about Moshlings, much less try and save them,' Zommer explained.

'Gah! Shut up, Zommer!' Hubbs snapped. 'Robots can change, you spiky-haired simpleton!'

'Oh, wait, that's more like it!' Zommer smiled sheepishly. 'You are the real Hubbs!'

While Zommer and Hubbs bickered, the Zoshlings had been busy downloading their scans of the space base.

'Got it! The weapon's control centre is located at the top of this tower,' Ooze said, pointing eagerly at the screen. 'Which means we'll need to go to this bank of lifts, here.'

The Moshis nodded in unison.

Chapter 7

SWEET TOOTH'S GUMBALL TRAP

The Super Moshis and the Zoshlings stood frowning helplessly at the door to the lift that should take them up to the weapon's control room. There was just one problem: the key that activated it was missing.

'Gah! C.L.O.N.C. has hidden the lift key,' Katsuma growled. 'Now we're going to have to waste precious time trying to find it.'

'Let's split up and look for it,' First Officer Ooze suggested. 'It'll be quicker that way.'

'Good idea, Ooze,' Captain Squirk said. 'You and I can check through this door over here. Splutnik and Dr. C. Fingz, you take the other door.'

'We'll search the lift bank for it, Captain,' Poppet added. 'Everyone meet back here in two minutes!'

'The Zoshlings have been gone for ages,' Furi said worriedly a little later. 'I hope they aren't in any kind of trouble . . .'

'Yeah, it's been waaaaaaaay too long,' Katsuma frowned. 'I think we should split up and look for them. But be careful, Super Moshis. We can be sure that C.L.O.N.C.'s Boss has dispatched some agents to capture us . . . or worse!'

'What's worse than getting captured?' Furi asked Zommer curiously.

Zommer shrugged.

'Getting your toes tickled by a Furry Heebee?' he suggested.

'They wouldn't dare. Would they?' Furi gasped in horror.

'I wouldn't put anything past C.L.O.N.C.,' Zommer replied.

'Anyway!' Poppet said crossly. 'Katsuma, Diavlo and Furi, you guys take the door Splutnik and Fingz took. Luvli, Zommer and I will go after Captain Squirk and Ooze.'

The door closed behind Furi with a loud ZWHIRR and the Super Moshis found themselves completely in the dark. Not a lamp was lit nor a computer dial glowing. They couldn't see a thing.

'Hello?' Katsuma called.

'Over here, Super Moshis!' two voices called at once. It was the missing Zoshlings.

'I can't see anything,' Furi complained.

'There has to be a light around here somewhere,' Diavlo grumbled. 'I'll just have a feel around . . . '

'Be careful, Diavlo,' Katsuma warned. 'This could be a trap . . .'

SQUELCH!

'What was that?' Furi asked worriedly. SQUELCH!

'Ewwww! I just stepped in something . . . sticky! Yikes, I'm stuck!'

SQUELCH!

'Gross! Me too!' Katsuma cried. 'My feet are stuck to the floor!'

'Don't panic, Supers,' Diavlo said. 'I think I've found the light.'

He flicked a switch and the monsters and Zoshlings stood blinking at each other for a moment in the blindingly bright light.

'Whew! There you are, Katsuma,' Furi sighed with relief. 'And you too, Diavlo.'

'Yeah, I'm here, Furi. But something gooey is sticking my hand to this light switch,' Diavlo replied. 'I can't fly anywhere.'

'Ahhh and there you are Splutnik and Fingz,' Katsuma grinned. 'I'm glad we're all safe.'

'I'm quite all right,' Fingz giggled. 'Although, like the rest of you, I'm stuck in this goo. What about you Sweet Tooth? Are you caught in this sticky mess?'

'SWEET TOOTH?' The Super Moshis all cried at once. For there, hovering in midair on a devilish-looking B.I.K.E. (Barmy Individual's Kitted-out Engine), was the evil C.L.O.N.C. operative.

'I wondered how long it would take you Super Stupidos to notice me,' Sweet Tooth crowed delightedly. 'And, for your information, none of you will be going anywhere! You've all been trapped by the half-chewed gumballs I've spread over every surface of the room. MWAHAHAHAHAHA!'

'Ugh! YUCK! These have been in your mouth?'

Diavlo pulled his hand away from the light switch, but the tacky strands of gumball held him tightly.

'Ahem,' Splutnik harrumphed. 'I think you'll find that not ALL of us are in such a sticky situation. I've tried to rise above the problem.'

Sure enough Splutnik, who was wearing his jet pack, had flown into the room and avoided the gooey trap.

Sweet Tooth's eyes almost popped out in anger.

'Blast that jet pack!' the candy criminal snarled. 'Even so, you still won't be able to catch me. That firework you're wearing on your back is too slow to overtake my B.I.K.E.! MWAHAHAHAHAHA!"

With that, Sweet Tooth turned to escape, flying into an air vent and disappearing from view.

'I've got this one, Super Moshis!' Splutnik cried excitedly as he revved up his jet pack and went after Sweet Tooth.

'Hurry, Splutnik,' Dr. C. Fingz called after him. 'The Doom Ray must be stopped!'

As Splutnik flew into the air vent he heard the sound of Sweet Tooth's crazed cackling echoing off the metal walls.

'Wow! It's like that creature's brain is a box of chocolates with only the nutty ones left,' Splutnik mumbled to himself. 'Well . . . maybe the soft-centred ones are still up for grabs too – WHOA!'

The Zoshling quickly swerved to the right to avoid a large gum bubble that loomed up in front of him. Sweet Tooth – that cunning candy crimbo – had left a gum bubble minefield to contend with.

'MWAHAHAHAHA! Watch out, little Zoshling!' Sweet Tooth shrieked. 'You don't want my gum bubbles to blow up in your face!'

'Don't worry about me, Dumb-Gum!' Splutnik called. 'I'm gaining on CHEW!'

In fact, Sweet Tooth was wasting so much time blowing gum bubbles that the Zoshling soon caught up to the lollipop lunatic!

Sweet Tooth's eyes darted suspiciously to the side as Splutnik pulled up.

'Mmmmmm, mmmmmph, MMMMMMMMM MMMMM!' Sweet Tooth said, but with a face full of half-blown bubble it was impossible to understand what the sugary villain was saying.

'I've got you now, sugar and spite and all things impolite!' the Zoshling cried. Leaning over, he popped the half-formed bubble, which exploded and covered Sweet Tooth's face with sticky gunge.

With riding goggles covered in goop, Sweet Tooth couldn't see at all and quickly lost control of the hovering B.I.K.E.

'MMMMMMMMMMMMM!' the candied creep cried, crashing loudly into the wall of the air vent.

'My work here is gum,' Splutnik chuckled.

When Splutnik flew out of the air vent the Supers and Dr. C. Fingz all gave him a rousing cheer.

'You da man . . . er . . . Zoshling, Splutnik!' Furi hollered, pumping his fist in the air.

'We knew you could do it!' Diavlo grinned. 'Now if you could just unstick us . . . ?'

'Try the sprinkler system, Splutnik,' Katsuma suggested. 'The water might help.'

Splutnik flew around until he found the correct control panel and switched on the sprinkler system.

'It's working,' Fingz grinned, lifting his feet. 'The gumballs are losing their stickiness.'

The Super Moshis slowly pulled their feet, paws and hands free of the stringy goop.

'And look what else the water has uncovered!' Diavlo pointed at a nail beside the door they'd first come through. A hook-shaped key piece was hanging from it.

'Hahaha! That's exactly where I hang my keys at home,' Katsuma laughed.

Chapter 8

A DRINK FOR TINY HEAD

I n another part of the space base Poppet, Luvli and
Zommer – following in Captain Squirk and Ooze's
footsteps – walked into what looked like the Space
Lounge Bar. It was decorated in moody pink and
purple tones, with low lighting and a portrait of Frau
Now BraunKau hanging in one corner. Behind a huge
curved bar they saw shelves heaving with bottles of
coloured liquids and cocktail shakers.

'This is my kind of pad, man,' Zommer said as he
checked out the funky décor. 'C.L.O.N.C. know how
to chillax in style.'

'If only they weren't, like, the bad guys, then you could hang out with them,' Poppet huffed.

'Yeah, totally,' Zommer nodded in agreement before noticing Poppet's sour expression. 'I mean, no, nooooooo, dude, I meant to say . . .' his voice trailed off uncertainly.

'Let's take a look around,' Luvli cut in. 'See if we

can find out what happened to the Zoshlings.'

Poppet looked in the corners, Luvli checked the counter and Zommer looked behind the bar. Neither Squirk nor Ooze were hiding there so he started inspecting the rows and rows of bottles instead, filled with Fizzy Milk, Spliced Slime, Wobble-Ade and many more weird and wonderful drinks.

'What's this book, Zom?' Luvli asked, spotting an open volume on the counter.

'Uh, it's full of drink recipes,' Zommer said, flicking through the pages. 'Gnarly! This "Stellar-Mix Burble-Quencher" looks rad,' he added, drooling all over the counter top.

Meanwhile, Poppet's attention had been caught by a piece of scrunched-up paper she'd found by the door.

'Hmmmm, this is interesting,' she mumbled, flattening the paper out on the counter and studying it.

'What's that, Poppet?' Luvli asked flying over to look.

'It's a recipe for a sleeping potion,' Poppet explained. 'I wonder if the Zoshlings –'

'Hey, check this out!' Zommer cried suddenly. 'It's the key piece we've been looking for. It was hanging up behind the bar the whole time. Sweeeeeet! Too easy!'

'What you think you doing?'

The Super Moshis froze at the sound of Big Chief Tiny Head's terrifyingly bad grammar. They turned to find him standing in the door, looking furious. As

usual the Hawaiian shirt he wore was almost as loud as his voice!

'You after key piece? Don't even think about it, Super Moshis, just do what I say or Zoshlings get it!'

As he spoke the doors at the back of the bar whooshed open to reveal a small cage. Squirk and Ooze were pressed up against the bars, staring sadly out at the Supers.

'Are you OK?' Luvli cried.

'We're fine,' Captain Squirk replied. 'We just feel a bit silly that we got caught in this stupid C.L.O.N.C. trap!'

Poppet turned to Big Chief Tiny Head and frowned.

'Well, it appears you have the upper hand – at least for now,' she snapped. 'What do you want us to do?'

'Make Big Chief tasty drink!' Tiny Head ordered, banging his staff on the floor for emphasis. 'You make special shocktail NOW!'

Luvli and Poppet exchanged knowing looks as Poppet's hand slowly closed over the piece of paper she'd found on the floor.

'We've got an extra special drink that'll make you sleep . . . er . . . I mean, weep with happiness!' Luvli said.

'Less speak, more drink!' Big Chief Tiny Head shouted.

'Sure thing, Big Grief Tiny Bed,' Zommer snickered

as Poppet passed him the sleeping-potion recipe.

'Do you think you can handle this, Zom?' she asked with a wink.

'Can a Tabby Nerdicat handle a calculator?' Zommer replied. 'Can a Caped Assassin handle knitting needles? Can a Skypony handle a harp?'

'Sheesh, I get it! You can handle it!' Poppet sighed, rolling her eyes.

'What can we do to help, Zommer?' Luvli asked.

'Bring me some Drinky Inky, Fizzy Milk and Atomic Hot Sauce and then step back and watch the magic happen!' Zommer chuckled.

Poppet fetched the icky green Fizzy Milk that looked decidedly rotten, the blue Inky Drinky with the skull and crossbones bottle that definitely meant 'dangerous' and the fiery red atomic hot sauce that positively screamed 'blows your head off!'. Zommer carefully measured and mixed the gross ingredients and twirled the shocktail shaker above his head like a pro.

'Are you ready for this, Twig Leaf Gingerbread?' he said as he poured the sleeping potion into Big Chief Tiny Head's coconut-shell cup. 'You're going to be sleeping like a baby!'

Big Chief Tiny Head frowned.

'Huh? What you say?' he asked suspiciously.

'He said you're going to be needing your ukulele!' Poppet quickly added. 'This shocktail is so good you're going to be writing songs about it!'

Luvli sighed with relief.

'Good save, Poppet,' she whispered as Big Chief Tiny Head sucked on his straw.

The Super Moshis leaned forward with eager interest. How long would it take the sleeping potion to work?

'What you all looking at?' Big Chief Tiny Head snapped. 'You never seen anyone with shrunken head before?'

'Oh! Sorry, Chief!' Luvli said as the Supers hastily tried to act casual. 'We didn't mean to stare.'

'But now you mention it . . . no, dude, we haven't!' Zommer grinned. 'So you had a run in with a Blue Hoodoo and it shrunk your head, huh?'

Big Chief Tiny Head nodded as he loudly slurped up the sleeping potion.

'This drink not bad,' he declared as he noisily hoovered up the last few drops. 'You make another!'

But suddenly his eyelids drooped and his shoulders slumped.

'Woah! Chief feel funny,' he slurred.

His feet stayed firmly in place, but his upper body began to slowly sway back and forth and side to side.

The Super Moshis grinned – the sleeping potion was beginning to take effect!

'Feeling tired, Chief?' Poppet smirked.

Big Chief Tiny Head nodded, then he stretched and yawned loudly.

Inside the cage both the Zoshlings began to yawn. Then Luvli yawned and then Zommer did too. That's the thing about yawning – it's catchy!

'Chief feeling very, very . . .'

Unable to even finish his sentence, Big Chief Tiny Head closed his eyes as his knees buckled under him.

'TIM-BERRRRRRRRRRRRRRR!' Zommer cried as the C.L.O.N.C. criminal lost his balance and fell to the floor with a loud CRASH!

'And that's that,' Poppet laughed. 'Good job, Zommer! That drink really packed a punch!'

'It wasn't punch, Poppet,' Zommer corrected her. 'Punch has fruit 'n' stuff in it. That was a sleeping potion.'

'Yeah, I know,' Poppet replied. 'I was just making a . . . never mind.'

'Now to free the Zoshlings!' Luvli said, flying over to the cage. 'I think this might do the trick.'

She pressed a bright red button on a nearby console and the bars to the cage parted, freeing Captain Squirk and First Officer Ooze.

'No wonder C.L.O.N.C. is so useless,' Ooze said, his stalky eyes narrowing as he looked at the snoring Chief.

'Sleeping on the job like that. It's a disgrace!'

Captain Squirk joined in the tut-tutting as Poppet grabbed the key piece.

'Let's get back to the others,' she said.

Chapter 9

THE DOOM RAY 3000

'Run into any C.L.O.N.C. trouble?' Katsuma asked as Poppet and her crew reappeared.

'Nothing we couldn't handle,' she replied with a smile. 'And you?'

'Things got a little sticky at one point, but Splutnik and his jet pack rose to the occasion,' Katsuma said. 'You got what you were looking for?'

Poppet grinned as she held up the key piece they'd found in the Space Bar.

Behind Katsuma, Furi held up the one they'd found.

'Then what are we waiting for?' Diavlo cried. 'We

have to get into that weapon control room. The Doom Ray must be deactivated!'

'I'll have those key pieces, please,' Ooze said, holding out his hand. Furi and Poppet handed them over and the Zoshling carefully fitted them together. 'Now I just slot it into place in this operations panel and . . .'

FOOOOOOSH! The lift doors slid open.

'. . . stellar!'

'Nice work, First Officer Ooze,' Captain Squirk said. 'Into the lift, everyone.'

'We're going up in the world, eh?' Zommer said as they skyrocketed up the tower.

'I feel like we're rising to the challenge,' Luvli replied, giggling.

'Yeah. And I wonder who or what is going to challenge us once we get up there,' Katsuma said, seriously.

'We must be prepared for anything, Super Moshis,' Poppet said. 'Anything . . .'

The lift came to a halt and the doors slid open silently to reveal Strangeglove and the C.L.O.N.C. Boss's giant

armchair facing a huge screen. It showed the Doom
Ray poised to melt Mount Sillimanjaro and a progress
bar at the bottom indicated it was nearly ready to fire!

The C.L.O.N.C. Boss was a little distracted,
though, bellowing at the top of his lungs.

'You are no longer worthy of the C.L.O.N.C.
name, Strangeglove!' he yelled. 'You ruined my plan,
you moronic moustachioed monkey!'

Strangeglove was getting a real telling off!

Zommer thought this was very funny. He mimed twirling an imaginary moustache and pretending to look terrified.

Furi in turn thought that was very funny and burst into loud laughter before hastily clamping his paws over this mouth.

But it was too late! The security alarm had been triggered and began to blare loudly.

WOOT! WOOT! WOOT!

With the element of surprise lost, the Super Moshis tore out of the lift and struck their battle positions.

Strangeglove spun round to face them.

'YOU!' he screeched, shaking his gloved hand in the air.

'Hurry, Strangeglove! Get them!' the Boss shouted, still hidden behind his armchair.

Poppet began to spin slowly on the spot as she worked her away up to an Up And Away Whirl. Katsuma raised his paws and assumed a kung fu stance. Furi and Zommer began to windmill their arms round manically. Diavlo gnashed his fangs and his boiling lava head began to steam menacingly. Luvli growled and her star-tipped stem unfurled, ready to strike!

'Did you hear me, Strangeglove? GET THEM!' the Boss roared again.

'YIIIIIIIIIIIIIEEEEEEEEE!!!' Strangeglove yelled

running straight at the Supers . . . then past the Supers
. . . then into the lift.

The doors slid closed and Strangeglove was gone.
He'd run away like the C.L.O.N.C. coward he was!

'STRAAAAAAANGEGLOOOOOOOOOVE!'
the Boss howled in fury, before slamming his fist on
the arm of his chair. 'It doesn't matter anyway, Super

Moshis! You're too late!'

His hand pointed at the screen on the wall. The progress bar had moved even further along!

'Cosmic catastrophe! The Doom Ray is at ninety-five per cent!' Luvli cried.

'That's right, Super Saps! My Doom Ray is almost ready to fire and I must bid you farewell!' the Boss guffawed, punching a button on the arm of his chair.

It immediately skidded to the centre of the room, where the floor opened beneath it. The Boss dropped out of sight.

'Great Galaxies! What just happened?' Dr. C. Fingz exclaimed.

'Strangeglove chickened out and the Boss bailed,' Poppet said hurriedly. 'And now we have to disable the Doom Ray.'

The adventurers stared at the giant magnifying glass.

'Ninety-six per cent!' Diavlo said, worriedly.

'What can you do, Chief Engineer Splutnik?' Captain Squirk asked.

Splunik sprinted over to a small control panel and ran a professional eye over it.

'None of these controls are for the Doom Ray,' he said desperately. 'There's no way to shut it off. The C.L.O.N.C. Boss has guaranteed that nothing will stop his evil plans.'

'Dudes? What's our plan B?' Zommer asked. 'We've got a plan B, right?'

The Zoshlings looked at each other doubtfully.

'What about a plan C? Or D?' Zommer grabbed

Dr. C. Fingz by the arm and shook him gently. 'Jumping Jellyfat! I'll even take a plan F!'

The shaking must've clicked something in Fingz's brain because his wiggle-stalk began to fizzle and he smiled.

'Captain! What about . . . ?' He raised his eyebrows expectantly.

'You're surely not suggesting . . . ?' Captain Squirk gasped.

'It's WAY too dangerous . . .' Ooze shook his head.

'Yeah! Remember last time . . . ?' Fingz said.

'For the love of Symphonia – someone finish a sentence!' Diavlo shrieked.

'COSMIC HARMONY!' the Zoshlings all yelled at once.

'Cosmic Harmony?' Katsuma asked impatiently. 'What's that?'

'It's the cosmic music we make – you heard it when we launched the *Rhapsody 2*,' Captain Squirk said.

'Oh yes . . .' replied Katsuma, unsure how alien singing was supposed to help.

'Zoshlings, assume positions!' continued Squirk.

The Zoshlings stood nervously in a semicircle.

'Ninety-seven per cent!' Furi shouted.

' . . . HARMONIZE!' Captain Squirk ordered.

As the Zoshlings began to sing, the floor suddenly rose beneath their feet as beams of bright blue-green light engulfed them.

The Super Moshis jumped back in surprise.

'It's out of this world!' Luvli cried. 'Quite literally!'

'Ninety-eight per cent!' Poppet yelled.

The Zoshlings sang for their lives and the more they sang, the brighter the light surrounding them became. Suddenly electrical pulses shot out of the Zoshlings' feet, lifting them slowly into the air. The weapon control tower began to shudder.

'I really hope Captain Squirk knows what he's doing . . .' Poppet whispered.

'Amazing asteroids! Look out the window, dudes!'
Zommer shouted.

The Super Moshis gazed out at the pulsating waves
of energy spilling out of the tower towards the Doom
Ray! The high concentration of Cosmic Harmony
waves beat against the magnifying glass until – CRACK!
– a small split appeared across the lens, then spread
rapidly across the face of the glass.

'The Cosmic Harmony rays have shattered the lens!' Furi cried. All eyes turned to the read-out on the wall. 98% . . . 97% . . . 96% . . . 95% . . . the numbers whirred down until they reached zero.

'The Doom Ray has completely lost power!' Katsuma shouted happily. 'The Zoshlings have done it! They've saved Moshi World!'

Chapter 10

COSMIC HARMONY

The electrical pulses holding the Zoshlings aloft began to grow faint as their song died away and they were carefully lowered to the ground.

'Well, that went much better than I expected!' Ooze grinned. 'We didn't blow up the control tower, the space base or Moshi World by accident – RESULT!'

Furi turned pale and gulped.

'Was that a possibility?' he asked.

'Oh, it was highly likely,' Captain Squirk said. The Zoshlings all nodded their heads in agreement.

'That was amazing, little dudes!' Zommer cried,

high-fiving the alien heroes. 'Your Cosmic Harmony rules!'

'And your singing was just beautiful!' Luvli smiled.

Just then, another screen in the corner of the tower suddenly spluttered to life.

'Oh, no! I thought we'd sent Strangeglove packing!' Poppet growled as everyone turned to face it.

BZZZT! SHKZ! CRIZZZZ!

The image onscreen gradually cleared to reveal the opening credits of the *Z-Factor*, the most popular talent show in the Swooniverse. '*Z-Factor*? This show, like, totally rocks!' Zommer cried enthusiastically.

'Really? You like this show more than East Vendors?' Diavlo asked in surprise.

'What's that?' Furi asked.

'Oh, it's a soap opera about a family that has a market stall in Albert Scare,' Diavlo explained. 'It's got –'

'Shhhhh! It's about to start!' Zommer cried.

And, sure enough, Simon Growl and his hot-headed haircut appeared on the screen.

'Zoshlings, that was . . . er . . .' Growl paused for a moment. 'Incredible!'

'RRRRRRRRRRROAF!' his hair eagerly agreed.

'So, how does a seven-album deal sound?' Growl continued.

The Zoshlings looked at each other in astonishment.

'Mr. Growl, you have our galactic gratitude!' Captain Squirk exclaimed.

'In that case you'd better get your astro-booty back to Music Island so we can lay down some tracks!' Simon Growl grinned.

'GROOOOOOOORRRRRR!' his hair growled.

'You Zoshlings are amazing!' Katsuma laughed. 'Not only have you saved Moshi World from being destroyed, you're about to become the biggest band in the Way-Outta-Sphere!'

'Yeah, it's been a pretty good day for us!' Dr. C. Fingz agreed, smiling.

The Super Moshis and the Zoshlings traipsed up the gangplank of the *Rhapsody 2* to a hero's welcome.

'We saw you guys on the *Z-Factor*!' Sprockett cried as the adventurers walked on to the bridge. 'You're gonna be bigger than Zack Binspin!'

'Pfft! I don't think so,' Poppet huffed. But she would say that – she's the president of Zack's Maniacs – Binspin's official fan club.

'Can I have your autograph, Ooze?' Hubbs asked shyly, his bubblehead turning a delicate shade of pink.

Meanwhile all the little rescued Moshlings were

busy crowding around the Zoshlings and taking
photographs with their Moshi Minifones and Happy
Snappies!

The Zoshlings seemed to enjoy the attention – except Splutnik. With every camera flash that fired in front of him, his eyes boggled on their stalks.

'Uh-oh, look at Splutnik . . .' Diavlo muttered. 'I hope he doesn't go crazy-locoooooo.'

'Leave this to me, dudes,' Zommer said. 'I've got experience in the music biz.'

He started pushing his way towards Splutnik through the crowd of eager Moshlings.

'Step back, folks,' Zommer hollered. 'That's enough autographs for today. The Zoshlings have to get to work and you Moshlings have to take your seats. They've got a spaceship to fly.'

'Ooohhhh! One more photo?' a tiny voice pleaded.

'Afraid not, Fifi,' Zommer replied as the cutesy Oochie Poochie fluttered her eyelashes at him. 'Everyone not directly involved in saving Moshi World, please make your way down into the passenger cabin.'

The Moshlings moaned disappointedly but allowed themselves to be herded off the bridge and led to the cabin by Hubbs.

'Good job, Zom,' Katsuma grinned as he watched the last of the Moshlings disappear below. 'If you ever want a change of career, I think you'd be a good celebrity bodyguard!'

'But, Katsuma,' Zommer laughed, 'I'd never want to leave the Super Moshis!'

'Glad to hear it . . . er . . . dude,' Katsuma replied.

In the engine room the Super Moshis watched as the Zoshlings clambered aboard their platforms and assumed their launch-sequence positions.

'Ready on the bridge, Sprockett?' Captain Squirk asked.

Sprockett's face appeared on a communication screen high on the wall.

'Aye-aye, Captain!' he replied.

Captain Squirk swivelled round to look at a second screen.

'Are our passengers all safe and secure, Hubbs?' he asked.

Hubbs grinned from the screen as a bunch of little Moshlings climbed all over his robotic body.

'Aye-aye, Captain!' he giggled.

'Then, Zoshlings, we shall begin,' Squirk said.

Suddenly wondrous music filled the engine room as the Zoshlings rose and fell in time to the melody.

The space ship shook briefly, floated into the air and with a SWOOOOOOSH! flew out of the C.L.O.N.C. space base.

'Super Moshis, we're going home!' Poppet cried.

Halfway through the flight back to Moshi World, the adventurers all met on the bridge.

'We owe you everything, Super Moshis!' Captain Squirk said, tears filling his little black eyes. 'Without you – and you too, Sprockett and Hubbs – I would never have found my crew members . . . or the key to the *Rhapsody 2*.'

'Or a new steering wheel for the spaceship!' First Officer Ooze added.

'If your Cosmic Harmony hadn't destroyed the Doom Ray we wouldn't have a world to go home to!' Luvli replied.

'And if you Supers hadn't pulled us out of that swamp back in the Unknown Zone we'd have been put out for kerb-side recycling by the Orange Hoodoos!' Sprockett chimed in.

'Oooooh, don't remind me,' Hubbs shuddered.

'I guess that makes us a great team, huh?' Katsuma smiled.

'C.L.O.N.C. should know by now: evil never wins!' Diavlo chuckled.

But before they could high-five each other, a loud alarm started blaring all over the ship.

RED ALERT! RED ALERT! RED ALERT!

Captain Squirk pointed out into the Swooniverse – at the fleet of Glumps headed their way, followed closely by a spaceship shaped like a top hat.

'It's Strangeglove!' Captain Squirk shouted. 'Chief Engineer Splutnik – ready our weapons and prepare for battle!'

GLUMPS INCOMING! RED ALERT! GLUMPS INCOMING!

While the Zoshings armed the blasters, the Supers and Sprockett and Hubbs rushed to a window to watch the enemies' approach. The Glumpanauts' little ships fanned out in attack position behind the *Rhapsody 2*. There were row after row after row of them. And at the very back loomed Strangeglove's menacing vessel.

'There are hundreds of them!' Furi growled. 'If only we still had the escape pod. Then we'd be able to join in the fight!'

'I should have known Strangeglove would be back!'

Poppet cried, glaring at his spaceship.

'Yeah! And trust him to be hiding at the back,' Katsuma snarled. 'That lily-livered louse!'

'Blasters at the ready, Captain!' Ooze called.

'FIRE!' Captain Squirk ordered.

DOOF! DOOF! DOOF! DOOF! DOOF! DOOF! DOOF! DOOF! DOOF!

Ooze brought the *Rhapsody 2* round in a wide arc and flew straight into the first row of Glumpanauts.

'They're returning fire!' Luvli gasped as the great gobs of Glump goo rained down on the Zoshling ship.

DOOF! DOOF! DOOF! DOOF! DOOF! DOOF! DOOF! DOOF! DOOF!

'Awesome shooting, Ooze!' Zommer cried. 'Those Glumpanauts and their goofy gunk are no match for the *Rhapsody 2*'s blasters!'

DOOF! DOOF! DOOF! DOOF! DOOF! DOOF! DOOF! DOOF! DOOF!

'Uh-oh! Here comes Strangeglove!' Katsuma yelled.

'I see him!' Splutnik replied. 'Make a Lunar Loop,

Ooze, and bring the ship round behind him!'

First Officer Ooze executed the manoeuvre.

'We're coming up behind Strangeglove now. Fire when ready!' Captain Squirk ordered.

DOOF! DOOF! DOOF! DOOF! DOOF! DOOF! DOOF! DOOF! DOOF!

Suddenly Strangeglove's ship started to spiral out of control. Fire poured from its rear engine as it began

to shudder and shake. The adventurers watched from the bridge as the giant top hat veered away from the fight and shot off into the Way-Outta-Sphere, a trail of smoke in its wake.

'Hurray! You totally lasered those Glump-o-losers to smithereens!' the Super Moshis cheered.

'You sent Strangeglove packing with his tattered hat between his legs!' Sprockett laughed.

'Yeah, that's the last we'll see of that C.L.O.N.C. creep!' Hubbs whooped.

'Hmmm . . . I wouldn't be so sure . . . ' Dr. C. Fingz

said, his antenna fizzing thoughtfully.

'Reset our course for Moshi World, First Officer Ooze,' Captain Squirk ordered. 'We have albums to record!'

As the *Rhapsody 2* approached Music Island the adventurers could already see the crowds waiting to greet them.

'You guys had better get used to screaming fans,' Zommer said. 'Simon Growl is totally gonna make you Galactic Gooperstars!'

The Zoshlings exchanged excited looks.

'We're . . . er . . . *totally* ready!' Splutnik replied hesitantly, trying out the new word for size.

'It totally sounds like it!' Poppet winked.

A cry of excitement went up as the *Rhapsody 2*'s gangplank lowered to the grass. The Moshlings were first off, running straight into the waiting arms of Buster

Bumblechops, who laughed with delight.

Next to appear were the Zoshlings, who were greeted like Roxstars!

But the sound of screaming fans increased triple-fold when the Super Moshis appeared in the doorway of the *Rhapsody 2.*

'Super Moshis! Any comment for the *Daily Growl*?' Editor-in-Chief Roary Scrawl yelled from the crowd.

'Just that we're glad to be home!' Katsuma replied, giving his fans the double-thumbs up.

'It's been a long and dangerous adventure,' Poppet added, 'but we've made some great friends we'll never forget!'

In the midst of the crowd the Supers saw Elder Furi and Tamara Tesla waving proudly. Beside them Bobbi SingSong and Simon Growl were arguing about the Zoshlings' burgeoning music career.

And right at the back, unnoticed by the Super Moshis and Moshlings, was the ghostly pirate crew of the *Gooey Galleon*.

'It looks as if everyone's turned up to welcome us back!' Luvli said, smiling and waving.

'We all here, Super Moshis!' a voice yelled over the noise of the crowd.

Sidling up beside them was Big Bad Bill, the nutty chief of the Blue Hoodoo tribe.

'We have big party planned!' he said, giggling happily. 'Blingo gonna rhyme and Zack Binspin gonna warble! And CocoLoco insist we gonna conga till dawn!'

And you know what? Even though they were very tired after their action-packed adventure, that's exactly what the Super Moshis did.

THE END